Happy Father's Day!
2018

Love,
Patti

Louisiana Wind

a novel of Louisiana

D1484815

Louisiana Wind

a novel of Louisiana

RANDY WILLIS

DEDICATION

To my three sons
Aaron Joseph Willis
Joshua Randall Willis
Adam Lee Willis
And my four grandchildren
Baylee Coatney Willis
Corbin Randall Willis
Presley Rose Willis
Olivia Grace Willis

Go now, write it on a tablet for them, inscribe it on a scroll, that for the days to come it may be an everlasting witness. Isaiah 30:8 (NIV)

CONTENTS

INTRODUCTION

"The best men I've known have been cowmen. There's a code they live by—it's their way of life. It starts with an abiding reverence for the Good Lord. They're taught to honor and respect their parents and to share both blanket and bread. Their words are their bond, a handshake their contract. They're good stewards of His creation, the land. They believe the words in His Book.

Learn from these men—from their stories of triumph over tragedy—victory over adversity, for the wisdom of others blows where it wishes—like a *Louisiana Wind.*" —Daniel Hubbard Willis Jr., 1900

This is the story of such men....

PROLOGUE

March 20, 1900
Barber Creek
Babb's Bridge, Louisiana

I'd give anything to be mounted on a fast saddle horse again. I'd give him his head and point him due West—West to East Texas that is. There, I'd buy another herd of Longhorn cattle, maybe even a Hereford bull or two. My son Daniel Oscar says I might have Bright's Disease and may never be able to ride and rope again. I don't believe it, not for a Yankee minute. He's studying to be a medical doctor. I told him I'm only a half-step slower than I use to be. Well, maybe a full step. After all there are more ole cowboys than there are ole doctors. If he's right, at least my sons will continue our way of life.

My name is Daniel Hubbard Willis, Jr. I remember well back in '61 when a mighty Louisiana Wind threatened our way of life, even our very existence. But first let me tell ya of a happier time. Oh, yeah, it was the happiest of times! Come to think of it, it was two years ago—today.

NARRATIVE

DAY 1

March 20, 1898
The Beef Pens
Mayflower, Newton County, Texas

It had taken us five hard days to ride to Mayflower, in Newton County, Texas, to buy 2500 rangy tough Longhorn steers, cows, and heifers. I preferred those crossbred with Durham and Hereford bulls. I'd made the trip every spring since the end of the War of Northern Aggression in '65.

But, this day I needed to fulfill a promise to our Cookie, Rooster, the best cook this side of the Brazos. I agreed to buy him a chuck wagon like my friend Charlie Goodnight had rebuilt from an army surplus wagon. I was slow to change, but it was time to move forward with this modern advancement. I would no longer need my hoodlum wagon I'd used for years to carry our food, gear, and bedrolls. Rooster wanted one with a water barrel and coffee mill attached. He also wanted me to buy enough soap, salt pork, boxes of bacon, dried fruit, flour, coffee, black-eyed peas, corn, beans, sugar, pepper, salt, onion, potatoes, lard, and sour dough starter to feed Robert E. Lee's Army of Northern Virginia.

After revising his list, I also bought assorted supplies from the general store to stock the wagon: eating irons, tin plates, bedrolls, tents, and, of course, a Dutch oven. Rooster also requested two bottles of whiskey for medicinal purposes, which I declined, knowing liniment and quinine would do. I did buy a white hat though, so everyone could locate me under the heavy longleaf pine canopy along the trail.

There was this fiddle and leather case just sitting on the store's shelf. Knowing how my youngest son Ran loved music, I bought it for him for his birthday. I also bought him three Big Chief writing tablets so we would have a record of this cattle drive. Then I hired twelve more trailers and a horse wrangler. We would need everyone of them to trail the Longhorns through the thick piney woods of Louisiana. The return trip to the beef pens at the railroad in LeCompte would take nine days.

My four sons rode with me: Henry Elwa, the eldest was thirty-one; Daniel Oscar was twenty-three; Robert Kenneth was twenty-one, and Randall Lee, we call him Ran, was only twelve. It was Ran's first cattle drive and his birthday to boot. He had read everything he could 'bout cattle trailing and cowmen. Like me, his dream was to be a cowboy. I'd told him he couldn't believe all that stuff about Wild Bill and about Elwa's favorite, Kit Carson. Now, Wyatt Earp that's a different matter, every word of that is true. I oughta know cause I'm a lawman too. Ran would soon discover the vast difference between a dime novel cowboy and the real deal.

It also afforded me the opportunity to share round the campfires each night the story of our family in a land of red dirt and tall pines. For, you see, Louisiana is our home.

And if that wasn't enough, it was the 100th anniversary of my great-grandfather's swim across the mighty Mississippi, riding only a mule to settle our family in what was then known as the Louisiana Territory. Oh, no, the Cherokees and Choctaws did him no harm, not even the outlaws. The same couldn't be said of a couple of plantation owners and a few religious folks. I thought surely we wouldn't encounter as many dangers as he had. I thought wrong.

DAY 2

March 21, 1898
The Beef Pens
Mayflower, Newton County, Texas

After bedded down in the home and barn of my old friend Wade Mattox who had died during the war, we arose at 3:30. Rooster had prepared biscuits in a big dough pan and coffee that would wake the dead. I preferred Arbuckle's coffee. Some called it six-shooter coffee, as it was said to be able to float a cowboy's pistol.

I reminded everyone that I had an unwritten rule prohibiting any man from complaining about another's cooking. Only a fool argues with a skunk, a mule...or a cook. But woe be to the cook who didn't get our meals done on time.

I told Rooster to pack up and move ahead to find a spot to bed down for the night at Burr's Ferry on the banks of the Sabine River. I asked Robert Kenneth to help him with that task. I told the others we'd bring them up and spread them out along the bank, with the lead cattle headed downstream. The leads get to drink clear water that way and as the drags keep coming they get clear water, too, because they will be upstream.

We packed enough jerky, pemmican, hardtack, and parched corn in our saddlebags to get us through the day.

We would attempt to make the first ten miles to the Sabine River, at Burr's Ferry, by sunset. I'd brought a dozen Catahoula leopard dogs, my Jersey bell cow Ethel, a remuda of horses, and six big rawboned mules for the chuck wagon from our home in Babb's Bridge. I'd also brought my biggest covered wagon to hold the calves born on the trail. I wasn't about to leave them behind for the red wolves and coyotes as some did. At first light we headed them up, took a deep seat, a faraway look, and kept our minds in the middle…the middle of that herd, that is.

We hadn't ridden but a mile or so when two young cowpokes rode up in a trail of dust. Eyeing them told me they might be brothers but they were also toting guns. I sure wasn't looking for trouble.

The older one asked, "Who's the trail boss?"

"You got him. Name's Daniel Willis, and this is my son, Elwa, our foreman."

"I'm Jeremiah Stark and this here's my brother, Jacob. Heard you were hiring back in Mayflower. We just missed ya. Sure could use the work. We've worked the drives out of the beef pens from Weeks Chapel to Toledo. We can rope, ride, and help ya with any outlaw or rustler problem. We get a tad bit more than other drovers cause we're known to be the best in these here parts with a gun."

"Is that so? How'd ya get those biblical names?"

"I reckon it was our mother, Celina Marie Stark, who named us," Jeremiah answered. "She died shortly after Jacob was born. Our sister Mary said she was one of those Bible thumpers. She should know, since she's one too."

"Boys, I've got enough help. You both look healthy but I live by a rule…no gunslingers. Don't get me wrong, we have guns cause I'm the constable back home in Rapides Parish, and my boys carry squirrel guns and the lot, but not like those .45s on your hips."

Jacob had a look I couldn't read.

"But, Mr. Willis, you have a Colt .45 Peacemaker on your hip too," Jeremiah replied.

"The difference is, mine doesn't have a dozen notches carved into its handle."

"To each his own. We're bunking over in Burkeville. Mind if we ride along until the trail veers off?"

"It's a free country."

I decided to let them join us for those few miles. Figured they wouldn't have time to become a problem. We were doing right well, I was riding point with Ethel. She was our "lead steer." Jeremiah and Jacob rode with us. Ran was riding drag with two trailers. Elwa and the other drovers were spread out in pairs in the flank and swing positions as the cattle stretched out in a thin line for some two miles. The brothers rode tall in the saddle, but those notches still bothered me.

We had ridden to almost where the trail forked to Burr's Ferry and Burkeville when clouds moved in. It was an East Texas thunderstorm moving faster than a ring-tailed cat with its tail on fire. I sensed the cattle were getting restless when all of a sudden a sky fire exploded nearby. My spotted Appaloosa gelding, Augustus, almost jumped out from under me. He was barely three years old and was still a little skittish. That's putting it mildly, I once saw him sidestep his own shadow.

Lighting shot down on the forest. The cattle spooked and started running through the tall pines at a breakneck pace. I yelled, "Stampede!" The other drovers echoed my warning. I also heard them yelling words they hadn't learned in Sunday school. My thoughts turned to my youngest son's safety. But then again that's why I had him riding drag…to appease his mama.

Jeremiah yelled to his brother, "Take cover behind those rocks and take Mr. Willis's bell cow with ya."

Jacob was headed toward a rock embankment when he called back, "Will do."

I watched him do some fancy riding on his cow pony as she dodged four-legged death. He needn't have worried about Ethel, she was already there.

The sound of those huge horns scraping the pines and knocking against each other gave me chills. The wood chips were flying faster than a hundred lumberjacks with axes.

My Catahoula hounds were trying to turn them. One had a steer by its ear and another by its tail, but they were way too outnumbered to make much difference. Jeremiah spurred his horse and was at a full gallop. He was able to slow them down enough to let me move ahead while I tried to circle them to the right to get them to mill by waving my hat. Milling cattle soon become exhausted, but they were hell-bent for leather. My plan did not work.

There were moments when I was sure I'd get crushed against the trees as the ground shook with their thundering hoof beats. If Augustus stumbled, it would be all over except the obligatory, "He died doing what he loved most." I asked the Lord to protect my boys cause it was now a matter of life or death. The prayer for our safety by my sweet wife before we left home echoed in my ears as loud as Ethel's copper cowbell.

The cattle stampeded through the woods and tore up the dirt like a turning plow. There was an earthy smell of pine that might have been enjoyable under other circumstances. I finally came to the conclusion that turning the herd was impossible. I figured that they'd wear themselves out. I figured wrong. Thank the Lord my Indian cow pony could run like a deer and was as sure-footed as a mule!

Then suddenly they stopped. No, it wasn't our cowboy skills. It was the Sabine River.

We'd passed Rooster with his chuck wagon. He was now about three miles back, but both intact. His six-up mule team was dilapidated looking though. Jacob had saved my bell cow, or at least that's what he told everyone. Ethel would never sleep with the herd again. From that day forward she bedded down with the horses and mules. I thought for sure my dogs had been trampled. Nope, they were all now cooling down in the Sabine. The drovers had all made it too. But what about my sons? All were accounted for, but were pretty scratched up, bruised, and a worn out bunch.

Ran was quite the sight, being covered with dust, dirt, and manure. He asked me if he could not ride drag again. He was unharmed and had now had his first baptism by fire as a cowboy. It would not be his last. What a reunion we had that night as we all sat round the campfire, except for a few of the drovers who were night herding in two hour shifts. We ate plenty of Rooster's sourdough bullets and Pecos strawberries from his Dutch oven over an open fire. Those biscuits and beans, along with his beef steaks, hit the spot. All that was lacking was my dear wife Julia Ann's apple pie, and, oh, yes, her Louisiana coffee made with the sweet waters of Barber Creek. I sure missed her. Everything tasted as good as a king's banquet and reminded me of our annual Willis Feast of Thanksgiving, for it was a day to be thankful—very thankful. What prompted me to share the most memorable Willis celebration I'd ever seen was Ran's comment, "Father, I thought you were a goner until I saw your white hat waving above the Longhorns."

"Not hardly, son...but almost."

NIGHT 2

March 21, 1898
Burr's Ferry
Texas side of the Sabine River
On the Middle Fork of the Beef Trail

As we sat round the campfire, on the banks of the Sabine, I shared a story that has been etched into my mind with the healing hands of time. It was in September of 1854. The colorful leaves had begun to fade in the mist of the autumn chilly air. I was only knee-high to a grasshopper, all of fifteen, but I remembered it as if it were yesterday. The celebration was the most glorious in our family's history.

There were songs sung and stories told. Family and friends had gathered as far as the eye could see. Some came by wagon, some by buggy, still others by way of steamboats on the Red River. Many rode horses and mules. And some even walked long distances. I'd never seen so much love or gotten so many hugs. It was the largest supper on the grounds that ever had been…at least in our neck of the piney woods.

The dewberry pie had a special meaning that day. Although, I decided not taste it in this particular instance, for you see it was my Great-Grandfather Joseph Willis's favorite. Just five days before, on his deathbed, he had looked me straight in the eyes and said, "I've preached on Heaven many times, but I've never done it justice. There's Jim Bowie, but with no knife. I see Ruth and Naomi. Oh, my, oh, my, it's Him!"

With that Great-Grandfather smiled, closed his eyes in peace and was with the One he had so longed to see. Oh, yes, there were tears of sorrow because we would miss him. But, there were more tears of joy, for you see, he was home…*home at last.*

DAY 3

March 22, 1898
Burr's Ferry
Texas side of the Sabine River
On the Middle Fork of the Beef Trail

Daylight was burning in my mind cause I'd slept to 5:30. Rooster had been up since 3:30, as always. We needed to make at least ten miles today, twelve would be better. The cattle were calm. Even their bellowing was music to my ears. We kept a keen eye out for injuries. But first, we had one not-so-small task to perform—swim the Sabine River. It wasn't exactly the swift Neches or even the muddy Red in Alexandria, but it was dangerous enough. The river was up two feet from the storm, maybe even three.

I'd been taught to expect the unexpected on these cattle drives. I'd expected the two dollar ferry fee for my wagons and even the twenty-five cents for Ran and his saddle horse. The six cents a head for my cattle was reasonable enough but there were too many so we had to swim them. We didn't lose a single head. But we almost did.

What I wasn't expecting is what the Stark brothers did. They took off their outer clothing and seized a thousand pound steer by its horns. He was headed down stream with a dozen or so head. The brothers turned him by his horns and swam across with him. The other steers followed. That was a feat I'd never seen or heard of before, except for when Great-Grandfather swam the mighty Mississippi on his mule. We then drove them some twelve miles without incident. Oh, in case I forgot to mention it, I had changed my mind about hiring on those Stark brothers, notched guns or not.

NIGHT 3

March 22, 1898
The Middle Fork of the Beef Trail
Caney Creek, Vernon Parish, Louisiana

After what I witnessed today, I wanted to learn more about the Starks.

"Now, Jeremiah and Jacob, tell me where you boys were fetched up? I'd like to know more about ya."

Jeremiah jumped right in. "Mr. Willis, we never got to tell ya why we wanted to be on this cattle drive in the first place. We're from Louisiana."

"Whereabouts?"

"Branch, sir, but our sister Mary now lives in Lecompte. When we heard that's where you were trailing your herd we figured if you hired us we could visit her. Her first husband, Charles Oliver, died in '87 leaving her with six younguns. Three years ago she married a young fellow seventeen years her junior named Arthur Allen Hanks. The age difference is a concern to us. We've heard stories about him, too, down in Branch. I told Mary don't be surprised if he runs off, but if he does he better run far—real far. They've moved to Lecompte to start a meat market. They now have a three-month-old baby girl named Lillie Gertrude. We so want to see and hold our little niece. We're hoping to live there if we can find employment."

"About finding livelihood, talk to Elwa. He's moving to Lecompte, too, to handle our cattle business. We need him there to make sure the Texas and Pacific Railway does what they promise. That's a story for another day. I'm sure we can work out something and you boys can spoil baby Lillie all you want. And, God forbid if Hanks should ever take flight with let's say a younger filly, he'll flee Louisiana for good once he sees those notched 45's on your hips.

"Nevertheless, our family will always be there for you boys, for Mary, too, and baby Lillie. Every single one us will be, from me to my sons, even young Ran. That's the cowman way. That's the Willis way.

"Now, one last question, who's your father and mother?"

"John and Celina Marie Deroussel Stark."

"Yep, I had surmised you boys were Cajun French. I love your people. Without them what would Louisiana be? The food alone was worth trailing cows through the swamps of South Louisiana after we lost the cause.

"For Cajuns, you sure can ride those Spanish cow ponies."

Jeremiah smiled, "Mr. Willis, we call them Quarter Horses. They can run like deer, at least for a quarter of a mile."

"It would appear they saved your lives today."

Jacob added, "Yes, sir, all our family seems to stay healthy. We had to shoot one of our kin to start a cemetery."

Everyone laughed as I looked at their guns again.

As we gathered round the campfire Ran asked me to share one of Great-Grandfather Joseph Willis's stories from days long since past. I thought of one he'd shared to father and me on a three day wagon trip in 1852.

Great-Grandfather and Miss Elvy had taken a little trip to N'Orleans on the Riverboat *Natchez*, in 1828. On the voyage back home they stopped in Baton Rouge. The French explorer Sieur d'Iberville had named the city after seeing a red pole that marked the hunting boundary between the Bayougoula and Houmas Indians.

It was there that Great-Grandfather met a young man who was headed home on a flatboat from N'Orleans. He caught his eye, being so tall. His face had a determination far beyond his years. He was mighty upset after watching slaves being mistreated at a N'Orleans' slave market.

After a spell, the young man asked his traveling companion, a Mr. Gentry, "Why doesn't someone do something?"

He then turned to Great-Grandfather. "You're from Louisiana, sir, and your wife says you're a Baptist preacher. Why doesn't the church do something?"

The young man continued to pour out his heart, "There are more slaves in N'Orleans than any other city in this country, and I hear tell that Louisiana has become very wealthy off their labors. I've seen men and woman shackled and collared, and treated like animals this week.

"I'm only nineteen, sir, and I know you cannot help the poor by destroying the rich. But, something must be done to stop this. I wish I could make a difference. I'm as poor as a church mouse with little education. My heart has been crushed by my sister Sarah's death this past January while giving birth. During this trip we've had to fight off seven men who tried to rob us of our cargo. We were just trying to make a living and then we stumbled upon a slave auction. Who am I to think that I can turn the tide in my own life, much less this scourge of human bondage? Have you ever seen a man with so many odds against him?" The young man asked.

Great-Grandfather replied, "Yes, I have, and I know it seems impossible, but with God all things are possible."

He bid him farewell, and asked the young man, "I'm sorry, but I did not catch your name?"

"Abraham, sir, but most folks just call me Abe."

DAY 4

I'd figured we had had enough excitement for one cattle drive. What I didn't know was it had only begun. One old man and two younger ones rode up to me at the break of day. The old man had a worn leather look. The cocky younger ones rode as if they were on ten dollar horses with forty dollar saddles. I wasn't in the mood for either.

"We're interested in your cattle," the elder spoke with a wicked glee.

"They're not for sale."

"We're not here to buy."

It has never taken me long to examine a horseshoe. Especially when all three had their Winchesters out of their scabbards. Nevertheless, it would appear it was hog-killing time and I was the hog.

"We only need a couple hundred. You'll hardly miss them. They're not worth dying for mister," the old man said with a smirk.

I told them there's three things I don't abide: cold coffee, wet toilet paper, and cattle rustlers. Just when I figured it was the end of the trail for me, Jeremiah rode up and took over the conversation.

"You try to take those cows and the only thing that's going to be missed is you."

"Don't I know you?" the old man asked.

"Yep. I know you, too, Scar Bartholomew."

"Jeremiah Stark! I thought you were dead. Do you think two on three is a dogfall?"

"My friend Sam makes it even."

"Sam? Where's he?" the old man snickered.

"Samuel Colt, right here—on my hip! I heard you were a lying, thieving Jayhawker in the war. Abe Lincoln may have freed all men, but Sam Colt made them equal."

About that time Jacob rode up. Just as Scar smiled again, one of his cohorts pulled his gun, Scar followed suit. Neither had cleared leather when .45 caliber bullets ripped through both their hearts. The third bandit was just a trail of dust by then.

This would be eighteen-year-old Jacob's first notch on his gun. I'd hoped it would be his last. My plan was to cut them loose when I first met them, but now, as my Great-Grandfather always said, "You've got to dance with the one that brung ya." I reckoned I would have had my last dance without them. We stopped the herd long enough to bury the scoundrels. I didn't feel like a cross was fitting so we stacked a few rocks on them. I had no words to say over them. Not any that would have mattered.

The Stark boys spoke not a word until Jacob asked me, "How do feel about all this, Mr. Willis?"

"There's a few men in Louisiana that need killing, but no cows that need stealing."

O N E

"A woman's heart should be so hidden in God
that a man has to seek Him just to find her."

—*Joseph Willis, 1785*

NIGHT 4

March 23, 1898, at dusk
The Middle Fork of the Beef Trail
Castor Bayou, Leesville, Louisiana

Now Daniel Oscar was from Leesville, so as we approached the town he decided to spend the night there with his wife Ella. None of us knew that when he invited his younger brother Ken to share some of Ella's fine Louisiana cooking a plan had already been hatched. It involved Ella's friend Eulah Rosalie Hilburn. When Ken first laid eyes on Eulah the welfare of our cattle seemed to be a faded memory.

After supper Eulah invited Ken to her father's farm just down the road a piece to see a horse she needed advice on. Early the next morning Elwa rode back to camp and informed us Ken's saddle horse seemed to have suddenly developed a slight limp. He would catch up with us in a day or two. Eulah's pony had a pedigree as long as her arm that was meant to impress. Ken was impressed. Not with the horse, but with Eulah. She was stunning, so he asked her if they could discuss the horse in more detail the next morning at the Hotel Leesville. They had an excellent café, with dark roast coffee, to start the day. He couldn't have cared less about that horse by then.

I later asked Ken, "I thought I'd taught you to always tell the truth?"

He replied, "I did, Father. I told her over coffee I would love to court her."

Ken added, "She seemed unimpressed and certainly not amused. She said she was only there for advice and was a lady that adhered to Southern traditions. She made it clear she did not wish to mislead me. I didn't have a clue what she was talking about, especially the Southern tradition part. The only Southern tradition I knew was on a horse with a rope or in a field behind a plow.

"Then she said, since she'd just met me, unfortunately she would have to decline any overtures of friendship, especially courting. That is, until I met her mother. Lo and behold, she then invited me to join her and her mother for breakfast the next morning so she could learn more about horses, and I'm sure her mother more about me."

Well, according to Ken, her mother started asking him more questions than a Baton Rouge lawyer. Eulah was as sharp as a tack and her English blood gave her a charm and grace like he'd never seen before, except when she exclaimed, "Don't ask any more questions, Mother. Cowboys love to brag about everything. How everything they do is bigger and better."

Her mother was not dissuaded and asked Ken, "Mr. Willis, just how many cows do you own?"

He told her 200. That wasn't near as many as she'd been led to believe by her Eulah Rosalie.

Ken began to sweat like General William Tecumseh Sherman in church.

"That's in my smokehouse," he explained. They both smiled and her mother seemed to ease up on him, at least for the moment. Eulah finally told Ken, "I'd like to see those 200 cows. Maybe even the live ones too."

Soon, I'd have another beautiful daughter-in-law. Albeit, with a lot fewer cows than Ken remembered that day. But, then again, I later learned that Eulah Rosalie knew more about horses than all of us put together.

Ran knew his brothers had heard my war stories on these cattle drives many times, but he hadn't, so he asked, "Father, can you tell me a story of the War of Northern Aggression?"

"Sure I will, son. I'll tell ya my favorite!"

It was in the winter of 1863 when a beautiful young southern belle got news that her handsome beau, a Confederate soldier for the cause, had been killed at Chickamauga. Her grief could not be abated. Each day she would read her Red Letter Bible and ask the Lord, "Why?" She got no answer. Each day she would take a photograph of him in his uniform out of her trunk, and tears would come streaming down her checks. As the months went by she had resigned herself to being an old maid.

At the end of the great War Between the States she would feed the men from the Army of the Confederacy who traveled down the red dirt road in front of her father's home. Many were barefooted, all were hungry. She did this to honor her sweetheart's memory. Finally, one day, her father told her, "Darling, we have no more to give."

She then would take her own supper and give it to those who traveled by on their way home to their loved ones. When her father discovered her act of kindness he insisted she stop for the sake of her own health. He added, "See, it's never ending. There's another."

As the soldier got closer, the young girl looked up, and suddenly stood, dropped her plate of food and ran down the red dirt road to the tattered soldier. She hug him, kissed him and practically carried him to the front porch.

"Now Ran, that was the greatest day of the war for the beautiful young southern belle and for me, too, for you see that soldier was me and the young girl was your mother.

"Rumors of my death had been somewhat exaggerated, as Mr. Twain once put it."

"Father, Mother told me that story, too. I so loved it, but she didn't mention the part of her remaining an old maid forever…I don't recall the handsome beau part either."

DAY 5

March 24, 1898
The Middle Fork of the Beef Trail
Castor Bayou, Leesville, Louisiana

We saddled up while wolfing down Rooster's coffee and biscuits. The Louisiana sky was ablaze with colors. A cool wind blew across our faces as we set out for hopefully an uneventful day. And it appeared it would be until young Ran followed his favorite Catahoula cow dog, one-eyed Jack, into the thick post oak.

The chattering noise from the underbrush was unfamiliar to him, but not to Jack. Suddenly there was a loud growl as a wild boar began to charge Jack like a runaway train. Jack attacked him like he was nothing more than a rabbit. The hog's tusk caught his belly and slit him from end to end, as he jumped.

Jack's piercing squeal echoed through the woods as Ran arrived on his mare. Rearing up his horse fell over backward, throwing him just yards from where the boar was pawing the ground like an angry bull. He now took aim at Ran just as I rode up.

Jack, bleeding profusely, got up, and this time went for the boar's hindquarters clamping his jaws on his tail—refusing to let go and allowing me time for one shot. I knew my handgun would not even slow him down. I took aim with my lever-action Winchester 73 and fired, hitting him in his thick skull, right between his eyes. The .44 caliber cartridge killed him, just a few feet from Ran.

Thankfully, the boar's tusk did not go deep enough to cut Jack's intestines or any vital organs. I'll tell ya, Jack has nine lives. He'd already lost an eye when he grabbed a mule by the tail. After that, I had wished he would not behave with such reckless abandonment.

Thank the Lord, that wish did not come true.

Daniel Oscar cleaned the wound and coated it with coal oil and Pond's Extract and then wrapped him in silver-coated bandages from Rooster's wagon. He had packed gauze with carbolic acid and wound dressings treated with iodine in his saddle bags. My future people doctor proved to be quite the veterinarian that day. He believed in Louis Pasteur's theory of germs. Others believed it was ridiculous fiction.

Ran laid Jack in the big wagon with the new born calves with strict instructions to him to stay still. He loved that dog more than most people. Today, he was not the only one. He then rode with the wagon and kept an ever protective eye on him until we camped. Jack would soon heal. All I could think of was, Thank you, Lord, and thank you, Jack. Also, I wondered what I was going to say to Julia Ann. It crossed my mine once, or maybe twice or maybe even more....

That night, Rooster prepared a rare supper of roasted pork over a fire he had kindled with wood. For some reason Ran had no appetite for pork, but he did take a slice to Jack. He refused it, too.

T W O

"I wish I could find words to express the trueness,
the bravery, the hardihood, the sense of honor,
the loyalty to their trust and to each other of
the old trail hands."

—Charles Goodnight

NIGHT 5

March 4, 1898
The Middle Fork of the Beef Trail
Burton Creek, Vernon Parish, Louisiana

"Father, please tell me a story about the good ole days of being a cowboy?" Ran asked.

"Sure I will, son, but this story wasn't that long ago. It's one that has changed my way of thinking about being a cowboy, and even about life itself."

As I was being fetched up in Louisiana I dreamed of being a cowman, so that's exactly what I set out to do after the War of Northern Aggression. Since I had no money I joined in "making the gather" in Texas. With the help of five of my younger brothers we rounded up wild and unbranded maverick Longhorns that had roamed free during the war. Before the railroads we drove them on the Opelousas Trail through the swamps to N'Orleans to be shipped north by steamboats. What we didn't sell we kept on the open range in Rapides Parish to begin building a herd.

Many of those were later driven to shipping points at Vidalia on the Mississippi and once to Shreveport on the Red River. The buffalo flies were so bad on the trail to Shreveport the cattle would run off.

Trailing cattle to Louisiana began long before they were trailed to Kansas by those Texas cowpokes. As early as the 1830s, cattle were trailed from Stephen F. Austin's colony to N'Orleans, where they fetched twice as much as they did in Texas.

Years later, I met an enterprising rancher that had also joined in "making the gather," named Charlie Goodnight. We were at a Confederate Reunion in Houston. He had been a scout for the Southern cause. Before that he'd trailed cattle to Louisiana. After telling me all about it he offered me a cigar, which I declined, and gave me advice on improving my herd through cross breeding with Hereford bulls. I knew I had to buy more high-grade bulls to build a better herd.

Goodnight invited me to the JA Ranch in Palo Duro Canyon, but then I got word he no longer managed it. He had a stomach ailment that almost proved fatal, too, so I figured if I ever was going to visit him I'd better do it soon. I purposed in my heart if the opportunity ever arose I would do just that.

That opportunity came in '87 when the Fort Worth and Denver City Railway was built through the Texas Panhandle. Goodnight was now ranching in Armstrong County near the Fort Worth and Denver City line.

But, first I wanted to see what the new XIT Ranch offered in the way of Longhorn bulls, maybe even a Durham. So, in 1888, I boarded the Texas and Pacific Railway at Alexandria and made my way to Channing, Texas, to visit the XIT. Surely I could find a few top-grade Longhorn bulls on their three million acres with more than 150,000 head of cattle.

If not, perhaps Goodnight would sell me one or two of his Hereford bulls. I trusted him. He was a Christian gentleman with an affable nature. I liked Longhorns because they were tough and rangy, but they were mostly long legs and long horns and not near as beefy as Herefords, at least that's what Goodnight had told me. I would then sell my culls and undesirable bulls. The new town of Channing was now a major shipping point so I had a way to ship them—my new prize bulls—back home.

It was a long ways from Babb's Bridge, but I finally made it to Channing. I didn't want to look like something the cat dragged in when I first met their range foreman, so I made my way over to the barber shop. I needed a shave, haircut, and bath. I sat on an old crate waiting my turn for a nickel haircut and a dime shave. The bathhouse was outback. The quarter for the hot bath would be the most expensive I'd ever had. The soap made me smell like a flower, though. I decided to buy some for Julia Ann, but I preferred our lye soap back home.

The old-timers were spinning yarns about the weather, the scourge of the XIT's and Charlie Goodnight's barbwire fences doing away with the "real cowboys," a cattle disease called Texas Fever and many a "she done me wrong yarn." Their laughter filled the room and everybody was smiling until one ole cowboy spoke with a gravelly voice, asking, "What was that young cowpoke's name? Ya know the one that got himself thrown off a green-broke mare on the XIT. That horse was a rank one, ya know."

"I was there. His name was Jimbo. He was a praying boy," the barber said.

"Not sure that pony was green-broke though, although that's what they told young Jimbo. He came strolling out of the bunkhouse one morning when some of the cowboys started poking fun at him. He didn't have much experience, but he wanted to show them he could rope and ride."

I took it all in and spoke not a word. I was spellbound.

The barber continued, "They were daring Jimbo to ride that crazy horse brought over from a XIT line camp. They couldn't handle the pony there.

"Those cowboys were real mean to him. At first Jimbo did a good job of ignoring them, but they just kept making fun of him. 'Come on, ya got religion we hear tell. You can do anything with that Jewish Carpenter's help, can't ya, boy? Why don't ya wanna ride that horse? Ya scared? Maybe you're too green like that yearling cow pony, maybe even yellow?'"

"Everybody gathered 'round to see what was gonna happen. Every eye was on Jimbo. His face was beet red. He just stood there looking at that horse and didn't move. The men laughed at him, threw up their hands and started walking away. He couldn't have been more than eighteen. I watched him throw his shoulders back and begin to walk toward the corral. He grabbed a bridle and opened the gate. You could hear the whispers as most of the men came back to watch.

"He bridled her and proceeded to rub the mare all over with a saddle blanket while he whispered to her. One ole cowboy yelled, 'Bite her ear.' Another, 'Snub her to a post.' Another, 'She's got crazy eyes.'

"Jimbo ignored them all, except to say, 'She's not crazy, just afraid.'

"Didn't take long for him to get a saddle on her. He climbed on her real slow like and rode with a new found confidence. She seemed to trust him.

"Suddenly someone cracked a bullwhip and yelled, 'Ride 'em, cowboy.'

"She must have jumped ten feet. And, as everyone hooped and hollered she reared up falling over backward on top of Jimbo. The horse got up but not the boy. He just lay there in the dry dusty dirt. I was the first one that got to him and he sure didn't look good. He tried to talk, so I bent down close to his mouth to hear his words.

"'Please get my Book, the one that boss Jake gave me.'

"First I thought I hadn't heard him right, but he said it real clear again.

"'Please get me my Bible.'

"I sent one of the others to fetch it from his saddlebags. I tried to make him comfortable, but there wasn't much I could do. Wondered how we'd explain all this to boss man Jake. When the Book arrived I show it to him. 'Here, Jimbo, here's your Bible.'"

"'Lay it on my chest and open it to John 3:16, please. Put my finger on those words.

"He spoke all raspy like.

"'Please, do it, please!'

"I found that verse and lifted his hand. He cried in pain cause his arm was broken. I placed his finger on the verse."

"'Tell boss Jake I made that decision just like he told me I should.'

"With that he closed his eyes and was gone." The barber had tears in his eyes as he ended the story.

I paused a minute, then said, "Boys, I made three decisions after I heard the barber's story. The first was to name the creek we now live on Barber Creek. The second was to have you boys bury me one day with my Bible opened on my chest with my finger placed on John 3:16. And the third was to give every cowboy that works with us a copy of the good Lord's Word. Your copies are in the chuck wagon. Rooster will show you where."

Jeremiah and Jacob seemed to be moved the most.

Jeremiah spoke first, "Mr. Willis, our sister Mary told us about that Carpenter. Is He for real?"

"Boys, He's as real as the skin on my bones."

"What does that verse say Mr. Willis?"

"It says that whosoever puts his trust in Jesus will have everlasting life."

"What does whosoever mean? Who's that?"

"I reckon, Jeremiah, that's you and me and every cowboy and cowgirl. Even the mavericks, the culls, and the undesirables. God swings a mighty big loop. But, there's many a cowboy that doesn't want His brand."

There was a peace in the camp as an unseasonable cool breeze blew in.

Then Jeremiah said, "I want His brand."

Jacob added, "Me, too."

DAY 6

March 25, 1898
The Middle Fork of the Beef Trail
Somewhere between Burton and Mill Creek
Vernon Parish, Louisiana

Two of our drovers from the night watch rode into camp before sunrise. A mile back they had found two steers mauled to death. Bear tracks were everywhere. Louisiana Black Bear were once sparse but not anymore. As a boy I learned they were agile tree climbers, unpredictable, and dangerous. I'd heard their charges were pure bluff. I didn't plan on proving that theory, though. I also knew he'd be back that night so I planned a trap. I'd used the leftover hog and a little honey as bait. Their sense of smell is their keenest.

Elwa and I hid downwind. Sure enough, one huge black bear came lumbering out for supper. Oh, no, not for the hog or the honey, but for me, and Elwa. Augustus saw him first and must have jumped twenty feet, but I was still mounted somehow. But, I had dropped my rifle. Just as I thought it couldn't get worse, it did.

Elwa drew a bead on him and misfired. I got the bright idea that the only other option was to rope him. Don't ask me why, I just did. Well, anyway, I'd read somewhere that a Texas cowboy once did that. Unfortunately, my loop went around his head. He threw me and Augustus to the side like we were rag dolls. I cut the rope and the bear took off into the woods. My bear roping days were over.

I was now ready to cook a steer, serve it to him on a silver platter with all the fixings the next time we encountered each other. At a great distance, that is.

NIGHT 6

March 25, 1898
The Middle Fork of the Beef Trail
Mill Creek, Vernon Parish, Louisiana

As we sat listening to Ran play two tunes by ear on his fiddle called "Green Grow the Lilacs" and the "Yellow Rose of Texas" I was transfixed by the sounds and the glow of our campfire. I also marveled at how quickly he'd learned these melodies on his fiddle.

One of our cowpunchers by the name of Gerald Duke had taught him the tunes while they worked their shift as a night herder team. As they circled the herd from the opposite direction of the other nighthawks Gerald would sing. His melodious voice kept the cattle calm. I suspected it was to keep themselves awake, too. Ran remembered each tune and later would perfect it on his new fiddle. He soon could play anything with a string on it.

When I first saw Gerald on his saddle horse Majestic, I knew he was a real cowboy. Oh, no, not by his clothes or such but by his open countenance and the way he looked me straight in the eyes. He was not innocent, of course; but living next to nature was stamped on his face. His vices had left no scars that the open range had not healed.

As Ran finished his tunes, Ken spoke up. "Father, I have a couple questions of my own tonight."

"Well, good then, ask them."

"I heard tell that you were part of the group that cleaned out those scoundrels on Jayhawkers Island. Some even say you had a part in Ozeme Carriere's demise?"

Ran couldn't resist chiming in, "My friends say I shouldn't even speak to one kid at school cause his papa was a Jayhawker. Were they that bad?"

"Boys, they were a bad lot, the worst of lots. It was bad enough they were draft dodgers and deserters, but when they started stealing horses, weapons, cattle, and food from our neighbors they became my enemy.

"Then, if that wasn't enough, when the Yankee General Nathaniel Banks invaded Alexandria in '64 he enlisted them to seek revenge on us. Banks called them Scouts. I called them murders, thieves, and conscripts. They burned our homes and even murdered civilians. They took advantage of our womenfolk while we were defending our homeland. No, I didn't shoot Carriere, I was in Alabama fighting in the Battle of Spanish Fort in May of '65, when Carriere was killed. I didn't kill him but a friend of mine did by the name of Colonel Louis Bringier. Well, at least his cavalry did. They cleared out the scum down on Cocodrie Lake's Jayhawkers Island.

"I reckon there are two reasons these rumors of my connection to Carriere will not die a natural death. After the war another friend, David Paul, was elected Rapides Parish Sheriff and then Mayor of Alexandria. His reputation had grown when he allowed no consideration to the Jayhawker varmints and exacted the most severe retribution. Sheriff Paul later helped me to become Constable.

"Those two friendships branded me as an enemy of the Jayhawkers. Don't get me wrong, I was, but the truth is I was with General Randall Lee Gibson at places like Shiloh, Chickamauga, Nashville, Badwin County, and finally in a Yankee prisoner-of-war stockade in Meridian courtesy of one William Tecumseh Sherman.

"Ran, as you know I named you after General Gibson. We should keep the name Randall Lee going to always honor my great commander and dear friend."

"Now William Tecumseh Sherman is another matter. On his so-called March to the Sea he burned our Protestant churches, including one that my Great-Grandfather helped organize. He being Catholic left them alone.

Bless his heart, Sherman ignored the fields of black-eyed peas while destroying other crops, as the peas were a major food staple of plantation slaves. Some say that the peas were all the slaves had to celebrate with on the first day of January, in 1863...the day the

Emancipation Proclamation went into effect. From that time on, they have always been eaten on January 1. I've never owned a slave, nor has any of my friends, neighbors, or family. I don't eat black-eyed peas cause they remind me of Sherman."

"Now, about Carriere. What really connected our family to him was an event that your mama will not talk about to this very day. Boys, she was living down on Barber Creek during the war when a young man attired in the uniform of a Confederate officer came riding up to our home. He had some thirty men with him. Because of his uniform she invited him and his men to come in for supper. She cooked for hours. After one of her famous meals, she provided them quarters in our barn. The next morning before breakfast she said a prayer and read a scripture to them from the Good Book.

"The young officer then gathered his men. As they started to ride away, he turned and asked your mama, 'Do you know who I am? I am Carriere, the famous Jayhawker. We were going to take your horses and burn you out. Maybe even shoot you since you said your husband was a Confederate.'"

"Why didn't he, Father? Why didn't he shoot mama?" Ran asked.

"As he and his men rode off he yelled to your mama, 'The words from your Book changed my mind. Anyhow, it would be such a shame to shoot the best cook I've ever met.'"

"Father, what scripture did mother read to him?"

"'For what shall it profit a man, if he shall gain the whole world, and lose his own soul?'"

DAY 7

March 26, 1898
The Middle Fork of the Beef Trail
Mill Creek, Vernon Parish, Louisiana

As the sun rose over the rolling hills through the trees I felt renewed and asked Elwa and Ken to ride point with me. They both knew they'd soon be riding point without me. Now it was time to start talking about how to carry on the business of making a living off a cow. The cow business had changed since I first mounted a cow pony. They wanted to expand with other breeds, maybe even buy some of them muley-headed cows.

We already had crossbred with Shorthorns from England. Those Durham's were alright, but I preferred Hereford bulls to crossbreed with our Longhorn cows.

Elwa spoke first. "Father, we want to buy a couple of Brahman bulls. We've got to do something to fight this Texas Cattle Fever."

"Go on, tell me more."

"Well, sir, it's your own friend Shanghai Pierce that says they're resistant to ticks. He believes it's the ticks that cause the fever. They also don't get the pinkeye. They can travel long distances from water, too.

"Father, we know you come from a generation that doesn't know much about these things. Education has come a long ways. Since The Texas Agricultural Experiment Station was established 1887, it's all about science. We understand your love of Hereford bulls, but would you consider a change? Ken and I have done a lot of research."

"Now grant it, boys, I'm just a hayseed cowman, but I did manage to pick up a thing or two along the way. I certainly don't know as much as your generation of educated fellers. But I did attempt do my

38

own feeble research about the breed."

"Really, Father, we didn't know. What did you find out?"

"Back in '85 I rode a train to San Antone to explore the ideas you boys have today. I stayed at the Menger Hotel because Robert E. Lee had stayed there. I was introduced to man there named Richard King. I later learned he passed away in the hotel just days after our meeting. He told me of his 600,000 acre ranch with grasslands along the Santa Gertrudis Creek. I asked him about his Brahman bulls that he'd bought a decade before down in N'Orleans and explain to him that's why I wanted meet with him.

"King had been a riverboat captain. In fact, he gave me a copy of a book written by another riverboat man that same year. The book was entitled *Adventures of Huckleberry Finn*. The author and King received a lot of their education on rivers such as the Rio Grande and Mississippi. Now, don't get me wrong, I believe in formal schooling, but never forget education is monkey see, monkey do. It should never be a substitute for good ole horse sense and the lessons learned on the rivers of life.

"Now, where was I. I first explored the possibility of buying a few Brahman bulls over thirty years ago after Richard Barrow had four shipped by the British government to Louisiana. That was in '54. But, thank you for the idea. I want you boys to decide, though. It's your decision, not mine."

"Father, we've talked it over and we think we should buy ten Brahman bulls from Shanghai Pierce," Ken said.

"Good idea. Your bulls will be at the beef pens in Lecompte when we get there."

"But, Father, it will take weeks for us to travel to Texas, make the best deal, and have them reach Lecompte by rail," Elwa replied.

"That's true, isn't it? I forgot to tell ya, I bought twenty Brahman bulls two months ago. They should be in Lecompte at the beef pens by now.

"By the way, Richard King also told me he had an idea that he hoped his descendants would carry out someday. It was to crossbreed Brahman bulls with Beef Shorthorn cows. If they ever do, he wants them to name the breed after the Santa Gertrudis Creek on his ranch.

"It never ceases to amaze me how old folks can still have a good idea. Imagine that, even an ole blind hog can find an acorn now and then."

"Father, we know you have great ideas. We use them everyday!" Elwa assured me.

"That's good. You know, they say Richard King's ghost wanders the halls of the Menger Hotel! I promise not to haunt you. Well, maybe if these Brahman bulls don't work out!"

NIGHT 7

March 26, 1898
The Texas Road
Big Creek, Rapides Parish, Louisiana

It had begun to rain as we sat round the fire. The smell of Rooster's stew promised some relief from the chill.

"Mr. Willis, Ran told me he'd lost two sisters and a brother. How did you deal with that?" Jacob Stark asked.

Jeremiah gave a stern look at his younger brother, "You don't ask questions like that."

"It's alright Jeremiah, I don't mind. After Elwa was born Julia Ann and I had two beautiful girls, Carvelia and Minnie. Then we decided it was time to have another cowboy. Elwa was about four then and we figured he needed a little brother.

"It was in January of 1872 when he was born. We named him David Eugene after David in the Bible. He was tall and lanky by the time he reached eight years old. He was smart and kindhearted like his mother. Just a month after his birthday, in 1880, Julia Ann and I decided to visit my father's home. He was a Baptist preacher like his grandfather and was now pastor at Amiable Baptist Church, which Great-Grandfather Joseph had founded a half-century before.

"On the way to Amiable for church on a beautiful Sunday morning Julia Ann told me, 'Stop the buggy, Daniel, I feel something is wrong at home.' I turned the buggy round as fast as I could and kept the horse at a trot. When we arrived home David Eugene was deathly ill. He had a terrible pain around his bellybutton and fever. I mounted my fastest horse and rode him into the ground with my boy

41

crying out in pain. I made the twenty mile ride to Alexandria in just a few hours, but it seemed like a year. The doctor said he needed surgery for he most likely had appendicitis. He added that the closest surgeon was in Shreveport, over a hundred miles away! My little boy cried, 'No more Papa, no more.' We had lost him.

"We buried him in the Graham Cemetery next to Robert Graham's home where I'd asked for his mother's hand in marriage. How could one place have so much joy, and so quickly sorrow? We now knew the unimaginable pain that Great-Grandfather Joseph Willis experienced when he lost his precious twins, Ruth and Naomi.

"During the funeral my father spoke words of hope—*Blessed Hope*. Julia Ann would later lie on his grave and weep for hours at a time. The next year we had baby Corine. She died a week later. I knew I had to be strong and pray without ceasing.

"Father's Amiable Church prayed and fasted for days. Then suddenly Julia Ann walked into our kitchen and told me that she had made a vow to the Lord that if we ever lost another child, she would never allow herself to grieve as she had for David Eugene and little Corine. She said, 'I owe that to our other children, and to you too.'

"The next day we walked down to the banks of Barber Creek. I told her, 'We should have no more children. Surely it's not the Lord's will.'

"She responded, 'Daniel, I love you, but you're wrong.'

"Two years later Daniel Oscar was born. When he reached twelve we told him of his brother and sister's deaths. His response was, 'We will never be without a doctor again, no, never again. I will study as long and as hard as it takes to become one.'

"Then Robert Kenneth, Ruthey Madella, Julia Coatney, and young Ran was all born. And, yes, we lost another. Precious Stella lived only four months. But Julia Ann kept her promise to the Lord, and our family too.

"Daniel Oscar is almost finished with medical school. He will be the very first medical doctor, and a surgeon at that, in Vernon Parish. A child with appendicitis will have a fighting chance, now. The Lord causes all things to work together for good!"

"I should tell ya, Julia Ann was a Methodist, up to then. After hearing of Amiable Baptist praying and fasting for her, she insisted on joining their church."

Elwa added, "She reads the Bible daily on the front porch while eating an orange. We joke sometimes that she thinks there will be no one in Heaven, except Baptists.

"When I asked her what religion Jesus would be in Heaven, she smiled with a twinkle in her eye. 'I reckon, son, it will be like the time a Catholic, Methodist, Presbyterian, and Baptist were fishing together down on Barber Creek. They got into an argument on what denomination Jesus would be in Heaven. The Catholic declared, "No doubt He would be part of our church, we have the Pope." The Presbyterian said, "No, oh, no. When you consider all that John Calvin did for the Christian faith, He will be one of us." The Methodist then spoke, "Nope, no way, look at all the Wesleys did for Christianity." The Baptist looked perplexed for a few minutes and spoke, "Gentlemen, I don't think He's going to change."'"

"Boys, you can see Jesus in your sainted mother's eyes. Through it all she still puts her hope in the *Blessed Hope!*"

T H R E E

"The reports of my death have
been greatly exaggerated."

—*Mark Twain*

DAY 8

March 27, 1898
The Texas Road
Big Creek, Rapides Parish, Louisiana

We veered off the Beef Trail onto the Texas Road to Lecompte.

As we crossed Big Creek a band of fifty or so Choctaw came riding up, hooping and hollering.

Jeremiah yelled, "Indians! Circle the wagons."

I told him, "We've only got two."

About that time they circled him. Jeremiah was as white as rice.

I had to say something, "Now, Henry you shouldn't scare Jeremiah like that. He's mighty good with a gun. You're liable to get shot.   And what would I tell your children? Better yet, my godchildren?"

"You're right, Daniel. Did you get that candy in Texas for them? They love those sugar plums."

"Sure did. Now I suppose you want the steers I promised you. Pick out the best five or so and invite me to supper sometime."

Later, Jeremiah asked me, "You do that often?"

"Every year."

"Why?"

"I figure I owe it to him. They were here long before us and, besides that, I'm not going to watch any child starve, godchild or not."

Jacob had listen to it all and asked me, "Mr. Willis, have you always been like this?"

"Like what?"

"A good man always doing what's right?"

"Not hardly. I've cut a wide path at times, not always good."

"Sir?"

"I'll tell you and Jeremiah a story of when I was a boy. My father was the pastor of Amiable Baptist Church. Once a month we'd have a church conference under a huge grove of cypress trees. The old men would testify with stories of their conversion. The womenfolk would sit by a pot-bellied stove, pray, and tell stories of mostly their husbands, children, and what the Lord had done for them all.

"There was singing, and shouting, and praising the Lord. And, there was plenty of food, but there was no fishing, swimming, or games of any kind for us boys. Now, don't get me wrong, that was all fine, but I had visions of a cane pole and me on the banks of Barber Creek with brim jumping into my lap. I thought surely that would not be a sin. After all, the Lord liked to fish.

"These meetings could and would go on for days. Being a preacher's son I was required to sit on a log that had been cut in half on the front row. To a growing boy, it was about as exciting as watching paint dry.

"Now, my brothers offered me a quarter if I'd livened things up. Do you realize how much money that was to a boy like me? I could buy two cane polls, with the line too. I needed that quarter.

"So, I got hold of my father's Bible the night before the conference and glued some of the pages together in the front of the big Book. I knew he'd never notice, much less preach a sermon that far back in his Bible. After all, we were a New Testament church.

"When Father stood up the next day to deliver his sermon he read the text for the day, 'And in those days, Noah took unto himself a wife.'

"I thought, *Oh, no, isn't that in Genesis?* All I could think of was another sermon of Father's, something to do with your sins finding you out!

"He then turned what he thought was one page and continued, 'And she was...fifteen cubits broad and thirty-five cubits long, made out of gopher wood, and daubed on the inside with pitch.' He held up the Book and added, 'My brothers and sisters, that's the first time I've ever read that in the Word of God, but if the Bible says it, I believe it! Amen.'

"The old men all joined in with an array of amens that echoed through the trees. I should know cause I was headed up one of them.

"Father continued, 'Just goes to show, we are wonderfully and fearfully made....'

"Now, boys, trust me, my father and a piece of hickory wood convinced me my Bible tampering days were over.

"Wish some of these preachers today would learn that lesson. Now, I know what you're thinking, but let me stop you right there. There's just not enough hickory in Louisiana for that.

"Since then, I've never roped a crippled steer or rode a sore-backed horse or changed a Bible verse to suit me....

F   O   U   R

"To write a good love letter, you ought to begin without knowing what you mean to say, and to finish without knowing what you have written."

—Jean-Jacques Rousseau

NIGHT 8

March 27, 1898
The Texas Road
Calcasieu River, Rapides Parish, Louisiana

After supper Elwa stoked our campfire on the banks of the Calcasieu River. He asked me to tell the story he'd requested every year since his first cattle drive.

"Father, tell me again about your first cattle drive in '67? I never tire of hearing it."

"And I never tire of telling it." I'll summarize here for you what I shared.

Just as I began trailing cattle, politics raised its ugly head. I'll give you an example of what I mean. I was once told a story of a woman who wanted to know what her son would become. She put what little money she had on her kitchen table along with a bottle of liquor and a Bible. As her son approached their home she hid in a closet. She figured if he took the money he'd chase the almighty dollar; if he drank the whiskey he'd be a drunkard, and if he picked up the Bible he'd might just be a preacher.

When the boy saw all this he picked up the money quickly and stuffed it into his pockets; he then drank the entire bottle of the Devil's poison, and finally he put the Word of God under his right arm and staggered out the door. The mother exclaimed, "Oh, no, he's going to be a politician."

I figured after the war the best way to feed my family was to be a cowman. Robert Graham's words when I asked him for your mother's hand in marriage, "Can you feed her, boy?" kept haunting my mind.

Within a year your mother was with child, and you were on the way. I knew I'd better get to it since the meager money I was earning from farming was not enough to feed a growing family. The woods seemed to be full of unbranded maverick cattle that had greatly multiplied during the war, but I feared some of them might have once belonged to our neighbors, so I joined in "making the gather" in Texas. There were thousands of unclaimed cows roaming free in that vast land. We were able to rope and brand 300 head on my first cattle drive. I had already registered my brand, the Bar-D-K, in Rapides Parish.

The next year Henry Warmoth became Governor of Louisiana. Now, boys, the last thing on earth I'd do is to speak badly of that low down Yankee scoundrel. Rooster's six mules dragging me across an alligator invested swamp couldn't make me speak disparagingly of that worthless Carpetbagger, no, not me.

Where was I? Warmouth was a corrupt politician of the worst sort. He promised to help reconstruct Louisiana. It wasn't about Reconstruction, but about taking advantage of us after the war, punishing the South through fraudulent elections and outright thievery. Out of all that came The Knights of the White Camellia. They said they would defend *our way of life*. I'm not sure if they were as crazy as the Ku Kluxers, for you see our family, being part-Cherokee, never got an invitation to join either. Wouldn't matter though, I've never cared for anyone who had to hide behind masks and robes to proclaim their beliefs. And, I certainly didn't need *our way of life* defended by whippings and lynchings. I trusted them bout as much as I did Louisiana's double-minded scalawag politicians.

Your mama's brother William Graham has a few holes in his sheets to this very day, and is proud of it. He says he's going to have his sons engrave KKK on his grave marker one day. Can you imagine standing before the good Lord and explaining that, and all those burning crosses they've used to preach hate? Listening to him talk you'd think he was the One at Calvary. I told him to come down from his cross, cause someone might just need the wood.

My friend from the war, Shanghai Pierce, told me a man could have all the cows he wanted in Texas with five million Longhorns roaming free. He'd driven a herd from Texas to N'Orleans back in '55 on The Opelousas Trail. The only problem was they weren't worth spit after the war. I got the idea that might all change, and change it did as folks decided they preferred beef over pork about the same time as Warmoth was impeached. Our beginnings were humble, but with it your mother and I fed you children.

Elwa, let me tell ya about that first cattle drive again. Demand began to change when a fellow named James McCoy established a cattle market in Abilene, Kansas in '67. The Chisholm and Goodnight–Loving Trails in Texas headed north, but were too far from our home to make it worth our while. Even the easternmost Shawnee Trail was not a good choice because of Texas Cattle Fever and the many drownings of livestock in the dangerous waters of the Neches River, not to mention our cattle would lose too much weight on such a long hard drive.

There was no railroad when I chose to drive our beeves to N'Orleans on the Opelousas Trail from East Texas. We crossed the Sabine at New Columbia, Texas. I could buy cattle then in Texas at $3 a head and sell them to the U.S. Army in N'Orleans for $20 a head. I never dreamed the selling price would double one day. We trailed cattle on the Opelousas Trail until 1882 when The Texas and Pacific Railway Company built a route from New Orleans to Northern railheads. The next year, when you turned fifteen, you made your first cattle drive with me.

Now, I'm getting ahead of myself. It was on my very first cattle drive that I met Etienne Fontenot. He owned a *stand* for cattle drives were The Opelousas Trail crossed the Calcasieu River. He once was good friends with Great-Grandfather Joseph's friend Jim Bowie, and Jean Lafitte, too. His way station gave drovers access to cattle pens, a soft bed, and a hot supper. I was fascinated by him for you see Jim Bowie had introduced Fontenot to Great-Grandfather many years before. He had become one of the largest land owners in Louisiana and planted the seed in my mind to buy land for our family and cattle.

I knew much bout Bowie from Great-Grandfather, but I wanted to know more bout Lafitte. As a boy I heard many a tale of him. The early inhabitants of No-Man's-Land held him in high esteem and he reciprocated by showering them with gifts. He was considered a war hero rather than an outlaw due to his helping General Andrew Jackson during the Battle of N'Orleans.

Fontenot had furnished his men with beef and supplies when their ships sailed up the Calcasieu River. Laffite made his Louisiana headquarters at his home. They became best friends. Once, when he admired a diamond stud Laffite was wearing in his silk shirt, he tossed it to him and said "Here, it's yours!"

It was during this time that Lafitte fell in love with his best friend's sister, Madeline. The dark-haired, green-eyed beauty had a charm and grace that the pirate had never encountered before. He was smitten by her soft-spoken ways and was hopelessly in love. But there was a problem, a big problem. She was already married. Her husband soon became jealous of Laffite, and accused her of having an affair with the buccaneer.

One day when her husband returned home from a trip he discovered she was wearing an expensive brooch given to her by the pirate. Furious with Madeline, he shot her and fled leaving her for dead.

When the news of the shooting reached Lafitte he vowed to kill him. The husband was never seen again. Some said he was food for the alligators. Others said Lafitte made him walk a plank into the turbulent waters of the Gulf of Mexico. Still others believe he made his way to N'Orleans and became a riverboat gambler.

Madeline survived and swore she'd been faithful to her husband. The bullet had hit the brooch that she was wearing and had saved her life. She never returned home after a trip to Lafitte's Maison Rouge mansion in Galveston to thank him for defending her honor.

One day they sailed away with his treasure. They're those that believe they were lost at sea. Nobody has ever claimed to have found any of his riches, not the gold, or Madeline. To this day some believe they have seen his ship on the Gulf of Mexico's horizon, not with a pirate's flag, but with one that has a pelican feeding her young with three drops of blood on her chest.

DAY 9

The Texas Road
Calcasieu River, Rapides Parish, Louisiana

We crossed the Calcasieu without incident. I knew the river like the back of my hand. But in the distance was a cowpoke watering his horse that I thought I recognized.

I asked Jeremiah if he'd care to take a little ride with me. He agreed and we approached the cowpoke with our Winchesters out of their scabbards. He almost started to flee until Jeremiah drew a bead on him.

Jeremiah yelled, "Do you want to end up like your padna Scar Bartholomew?"

We tied him up in the big wagon with the calves, for the nearest jail was in Alexandria. We were not far from my home in Babb's Bridge. I left Elwa in charge and rode home for the night, with the outlaw in tow. Julia Ann met me at door.

How excited she was and asked, "Who's your *friend*?"

I told her and added, "He will be sleeping tonight handcuffed to the foot of our iron bed cause he might get loose tied to a tree."

I told the outlaw, "I'd better not hear a sound out of you tonight. If I do, I'll do more than just tie you to a tree."

Jeremiah asked, "How'd you sleep?"

"Like a baby."

"Well, how'd your wife sleep?"

"Not a wink. I can't imagine what kept her awake."

I needed to get back to the herd so I sent a wire from Forest Hill's telegraph station to the Sheriff. They would need to pick him up when we got to Lecompte. I had no time to ride to Alex.

NIGHT 9

March 28, 1898
The Texas Road
Spring Creek, Rapides Parish, Louisiana

As we approached the trails end Jeremiah asked me, "Mr. Willis, a ways back you mentioned a story about the Texas and Pacific Railway that was for another time. We're almost there. Is that a story you'd be willing to share?"

"Not only willing, but if you're going to work with us you need to know it." First, I want to tell ya, there are those that say there are no honest lawyers. That's simply not true. Don't you believe a word of it. Just last year I met one in Mississippi and asked him to move to Louisiana so we'd have one. Here's that story."

In Louisiana the railroad is responsible for the health and wellbeing of our cattle once they are shipped north. That's the law and it's a good one cause at the end of the trail we can ride home and not worry bout them again. At least that's what I thought.

In the spring of '83 I decided to trail 600 head of Longhorn cattle from East Texas to Lecompte. Elwa was just a pup then, all of fifteen, but he'd told me he could rope and ride like one of those Mexican vaqueros he'd read bout. I'd read those stories, too, and told him, "Good, cause they say they only dismount for a chance to dance with pretty girls. And since there's no pretty girls along the trail, you will have to sleep in your saddle."

The Texas and Pacific Railroad, called the T&P today, had finished a route from Shreveport to New Orleans the previous September. We would no longer need to trail cattle through the treacherous swamp country from East Texas to New Orleans. We never drove a single head on the Opelousas Trail again after the railroad came to Lecompte. From that day forward we've driven our cattle on the Beef and Texas roads.

The cattle drive went well. I'd told Elwa he could dismount anytime he wished, pretty girls or not. After we drove the longhorns into the railroad's beef pens we were eager to get home to a soft bed and the loving arms of our family.

Two weeks later I got word that sixty head of our cattle were dead. In fact the herd was still in the railroad's beef pen cause of the large number of cattle being shipped from the railheads north of Lecompte, at least that's what they claimed. I rode over to discuss the matter. They informed me their lawyers had said the cattle were not their responsibility until they were loaded onto the train. I gave them the most educated response I could muster for their lawyers: "Hog wash." Trust me a few other words came to mind, but discretion got the best of me.

I rode straight from there to Alex and hired me a lawyer. He filed a lawsuit and the judge ruled in my favor.

Jeremiah made a good point, "But Mr. Willis, was not the judge a lawyer, too? Was he not honest?"

I stood corrected by Jeremiah. I apologized in sackcloth and ashes for falsely accusing all Louisiana lawyers of being dishonest. I was wrong. "Did I ever tell ya bout the time I was in Mississippi and met two honest lawyers?"

DAY 10

March 29, 1898
Trails End
The Railroad Cattle Pens
Lecompte, Louisiana

I'd made a promise the day before to the mayor when I was at the telegraph station in Forest Hill. He saw me and suggested I drive the Longhorns down the main street of Forest Hill. He said the kids would love it and the not-so-young kids, too. As we approached the town, the streets were lined with people. The Longhorns were as docile as kittens as we moved through main street. Of course Ethel led the way. She looked as proud as a peacock. I asked Ran to join me as the point cowman. We could hear young boys tell their mothers, "I want to be a cowboy."

Now, the good mayor also suggested that we have a Willis Feast of Celebration after we drove our cattle to the beef pens in LeCompte. We were less than a day away, so I agreed. It would be a wonderful way to say thank you to our cowhands and our neighbors. No neighbor of ours had "accidently" put the wrong brand on a single head of our cows.

NIGHT 10

March 29, 1898
Trails End
The Railroad Cattle Pens
Lecompte, Louisiana

"Father, being at the railroad again reminds me of that trip you and mama took to New Orleans," Elwa said.

"I suppose the others might want to know what you're talking bout." I can tell ya it was just six years ago on a hot August night in 1892. Your mother wanted to see N'Orleans. Being fetched up in Jackson Parish, N'Orleans was like a different country to her. I told her it would be that way even if she was from Baton Rouge.

"She'd never ridden a train either, so we boarded the Texas and Pacific Railway just across the tracks from here. I hid $2,000 on me just in case I was able to buy a few prized bulls at auction while we were there. I didn't trust the train's safe, and banks even less.

"After dinner in a fancy dining car we watched with amazement the abundance of wildlife along the tracks. The old plantations reminded me of a time we'd never know again. It was in the dining car that we met a school teacher named Eugene Bunch. Julia Ann told him all about our Eugene. He got tears in his eyes. He was a Southern gentleman, except maybe when he found out I was a cowman and asked, 'You must be wealthy?' Now, boys, we have always been taught not to talk about such things and never do anything that was a show of wealth, so I replied, 'Not hardly, we're just trying to feed our children and pay half the rent.'

"He laughed and excused himself so fast you'd thought the train was on fire. Julia Ann said, 'Now Daniel, that's how I hope our boys turn out. What a polite Christian gentleman.'

"Then suddenly the train came to an abrupt stop when a dozen or so men appeared on the tracks heavily armed. As they boarded,

Mr. Bunch stood and introduced himself as Captain J. F. Gerard to the passengers. Your mother looked like she'd just heard a dog talk. He then politely tipped his hat to the ladies, while refusing to take their purses, and he was very polite while taking the wallets of all the men, all except mine. When he got to me, he told his gang, 'Don't waste your time here, he doesn't even have enough to pay half his rent.'

"I later heard he managed to steal $78 from the other passages. That ended our trip, for your mother said, 'I've seen enough, take me home.' I knew I needed to find a fast horse with a buggy or a train headed in the opposite direction. I couldn't help but say, 'He was such a polite Christian gentleman. I hope our boys turn out that way.' She did not find the humor in my words, but after a brief hesitation said, 'Daniel, do you have any idea how it feels to be thrown off a moving train?' I could see that twinkle in her eyes, which always meant it's alright."

"A few weeks later Pinkerton detectives tracked Bunch to a swamp near Franklin, Louisiana, and shot him dead along with all his gang.

DAY 11

March 30, 1898
The Willis Feast of Celebration
Daniel Willis's Home on Barber Creek
Babb's Bridge Louisiana

We had a huge bonfire to illuminate the celebration and take the chill out of the air. I also had decided to have fireworks. The kids were very excited, and me too. You might say it was a day of *expositive excitement*, not cause of the fireworks, though. At least not the kind I lit with a piece of kindling from our bonfire.

The spark to these fireworks was kindled all the way back when I married Julia Ann. After we got married my brothers started to marry Julia Ann's sisters. Not one, not two, but three of them. Four Willis brothers, in all, married to four Graham sisters.

The problem arose when my brother Matthew decided to make it five. He set out to win Julia Ann's youngest sister Lucy Ruth Graham's affection.

She told him, "No, Matthew, I'm in love with James Moore."

Now, that was alright with Matthew. He then got word from one of the other sisters that was not the reason. She confided that Lucy had told the entire Graham clan that Matthew was just too ugly to marry. That was alright with Matthew, too…until he commandeered a bottle of *Sweet Lucy*, no pun intended. The white lightning could peal the paint off Rooster's chuck wagon. If that was not enough, Lucy had asked our father if he would marry her and Mr. Moore. He agreed!

Now the stage was set for the most exciting Willis Feast of Celebration ever. No sooner than father had said grace here came Matthew on his horse hooping and hollering words that I've chosen to forget. I figured, let him ride through and sleep it off down on

Barber Creek, but he wasn't done. He had obviously noticed Lucy and James's table on his first ride through.

Here he came again! Julia Ann cried out, "Do something, Daniel."

So, I did. Now grant it I was a tad bit slower than I used to be when I could jump a four rail fence with a bail of cotton on my back. But, I wasn't thinking bout that as I jumped on the back of the closest horse and rode like I was eighteen again. I grabbed his horse's bridle and turned the mare in a tight circle.

The circle was too tight for Matthew. He landed face down in a chocolate cake Lucy had baked. I figured it would be the last piece of cake he'd ever have of hers, so I told him, "You might as well eat the rest." He thanked her and told her he preferred her sisters' cakes, though. She did not get the gist of his remarks.

I felt at least the fireworks were over. Then I saw father. His opinion of anything stronger than dark roast Louisiana coffee was somewhere in vicinity of the Devil, himself, playing the Wedding March, on Ran's fiddle.

I walked with Matthew down to Barber Creek to wash him up a little. When he cried my heart broke for him, but I knew he'd someday meet another that would catch his fancy, albeit I also knew it would never be one of the Graham sisters, not even a cousin, not even a distant cousin. In fact, he might consider a different Parish where there were no Grahams.

I told him, "It's just puppy love."

He responded, "It's real to this puppy!"

What the healing hands of time could not mend, eventually the arms of another did. Matthew never drank alcohol or ate chocolate cake again, at least not face down.

F I V E

"There's a Rider coming on a magnificent steed, a white horse, I'm told. He knows all the brands and earmarks, for you see He owns the cattle on a thousand hills. He will separate the goats from His sheep. If you listen carefully, you might even hear hoofbeats, for you see He's mounted even as I speak. Not even a Louisiana Wind can change the fact that He's coming—*coming again!*"

—*Daniel Hubbard Willis Jr., 1900*

EPILOGUE

April 15, 1900
Easter Sunday
Babb's Bridge, Louisiana on Barber Creek
Excerpted from Randall "Ran" Lee Willis's Diary

Father had taught me much about being a cowman, and about life, too. He encouraged me to write it all down on my Big Chief writing tablets he'd bought me. He said it was so that, "Those that come after us might not make the same mistakes."

I heard tell the crappie were biting down on Cocodrie Lake. But, this being Easter they'd just have to wait to jump into my boat. Our Dominicker rooster's crowing reminded me I should start loading the wagon for church. I was truly excited, for father had been asked to speak that day at Amiable Baptist. Father was frail but up to the task. There would be a huge supper on the grounds after church.

I'd told mama we should have Easter eggs. A friend of mine from Spring Hill Academy told me all bout them.

He said, "When my folks lived in Germany, they decorated eggs at Easter."

Mama replied, "That will never catch on here. The hens would revolt, and me, too."

"Mama, they hid them, too."

She looked puzzled and asked, "Why in the world would they do that? Were they that ugly?"

"Not to worry, Mama, a rabbit then helps them find the eggs."

"Son, I'm going down to that school tomorrow and see if they've been into the cooking sherry."

I quickly changed the conversation. "Mama, what did you bake for the supper on the grounds?"

"Apple pie, of course. And, your father has butchered a hog, so were taking a smoked ham from our smokehouse, too. You know son, Baptists love to eat. Some I know are digging their grave with a fork."

Mother then added, "You know your Grandpa Daniel, Sr. was the pastor there for many years. He died a year and a week, to the day, after you were born. He was cut from the same cloth as his Grandfather Joseph Willis, and he even planted more churches than he did. He was the best man I ever knew. It was his words of wisdom from the Book that gave me strength to go on after the deaths of your brother and sisters."

As our wagon rolled down the red dirt road I could see the church steeple pointing toward Heaven. It would forever remind me of Father's words that day. As the folks gathered, father arose and slowing walked to the front of the crowd. Elwa held his arm to steady him. He spoke with a frail voice.

"Now, friends, as you know, I'm no preacher. But, I've been asked to speak a few words of my father, who is buried a few yards from here.

"But, then again, he's not there. Now, some of ya might be thinking that's not true. You might say, I was at his funeral. Others of you saw him in his open casket. A few of you helped lower his pine box in the ground, shoveled dirt on it, too.

"I can only explain why I believe that by using his own words about the loss of his Preacher. If you don't mine, I'll read them.

"'It was a sad day—the saddest day ever. For you see our Country Preacher had died. I trusted him. I'd staked my future on him. But now he was extinguished like a flickering candle in the wind. The young Preacher's enemies, and there were many, had won. Success had eluded him, for you see he didn't have enough money even for a grave, much less a marker. Fortunately, a kind soul gave him one. The womenfolk buried him on a Friday, for you see none of the men could be found, save one.

"'Oh, yes, he'd made some promises, big ones too. The kind no man could keep. But, he now had faded as the autumn colors. As victors, his enemies would surely exact revenge on his friends, so they hid like rabbits in a hole. One broke his promise and denied him. Still another betrayed him. Many others even hated him. He was rejected by the religious folk of that day.

"'The woman didn't seem to be afraid though, and three days later went to the cemetery to tend to him. But, he was not there, for you see the Country Preacher had risen, just as He said he would. One of the woman told his followers he was alive. After seeing all he'd done, one of friends even doubted that.'

"Today, many doubt that story, too, but I don't. Now, my friends, that's why I know my father is not in that grave cross the road. Because if it could not hold that Country Preacher, it cannot hold my father, or me one day in the not so distant future. He had taken death, the grave, and even Hell captive. I have but three words to say. They're the three greatest words ever spoken: 'He is risen.'"

As father ended his words, mother stood and began to sing, "Low in the grave he lay, Jesus my Savior." We all joined in, "Up from the grave he arose; with a mighty triumph o'er his foes. He arose a victor from the dark domain, and he lives forever, with his saints to reign. He arose! He arose! Hallelujah! Christ arose!"

Yes, I was the first in line for mama's apple pie…but first I accepted the truth of my father's words when I walked to the front of that church and knelt and asked Christ to come into my life and take over. For, you see, he arose for me, too, and you, too!

Suddenly watching paint dry was exciting to me….

Appendix A

Historical Characters

Daniel Hubbard Willis Jr.–Great-Grandson of Reverend Joseph Willis. Cowman, Spring Hill area in Rapides Parish Constable, and Confederate veteran. He fought in many of the great battles of the Civil War, including Shiloh, Bull Run, Perryville, Murfreesboro, Missionary Ridge, and Chickamauga.

An excerpt from his obituary in the *Alexandria Town Talk*, on June 23, 1900, stated:

"He participated in all the hard battles of that army and for bravery, soldierly bearing, discipline and devotion to duty, he was unexcelled in his entire Brigade. He was made Orderly Sergeant of his Company at an early period of the war. It has always been said by his surviving comrades that when any particularly dangerous service was required, such as scouting parties to ascertain the position and movements of the enemy, he was always selected for the place, and never hesitated to go, let the danger be what it may.

"He was for a long time connected with the famous Washington Artillery, and at the battle of Chickamauga so many horses of the battery to which he was attached were killed that they had to pull the guns off the field by hand to keep them from falling in the hands of the enemy.

"He was paroled at Meridian, Miss., in May of 1865, and brought home with him a copy of General Gibson's farewell address to his soldiers and of him it can be truly said that through the remaining years of his life he followed the advice then given by his beloved commander. His love for the Southern cause, and for the men who wore the gray, was not dimmed by years, but he lived and died firmly convinced of the justice of the cause for which the South poured out so much of her best blood and treasure.

"Before death he expressed a wish that he might see his children who were at home, especially Randall L., his baby boy, whom he had named in honor of his beloved Brigadier General, Randall Lee Gibson. He also requested that his Confederate badge be pinned on his breast and buried with him."

The writer of his obituary added, "During an intimate acquaintance, covering a period of twenty-five years, the writer never heard a vulgar or profane word pass his lips."

✭   ✭   ✭

He was the first of four Willis brothers to marry four Graham sisters. He married Julia Ann Graham on January 5, 1867. He affectingly called her Julie Ann.

When he asked her father, Robert Graham, for her hand in marriage he responded, "Can you feed her?" Daniel replied, "I have a horse, a milk cow, a barrel of corn and a barrel of molasses." Robert exclaimed, "My goodness, son, you have enough to marry several of my daughters." They were married at Robert's home, near Forest Hill, Louisiana, on Barber Creek.

Just a year later, on January 16, 1868, Daniel sold Robert Graham, 119 acres, "In the fork of Barber Creek," for $350.00. A sum that would have been almost a year's wages at the time. When Daniel died, in 1900, he left Julia Ann, $35,000.00 in gold (the equivalent of $980,000.00 today), a home, land, and the woods full of cows, hogs, and horses on Barber Creek. She lived thirty-six years after his death. She never remarried and provided for her family, even through the Great Depression. Daniel had made good his promise to "feed" Julia Ann…and then some.

After being made Constable of the Spring Hill area, in Rapides Parish, Julia Ann often spoke of the time he captured an outlaw from Texas who was hid out in the piney woods of Louisiana. She said it was too late to make the trip on horseback to the jail, in Alexandria. Therefore Daniel handcuffed the outlaw to the foot of their bed for the overnight stay. He then told the outlaw, "you better not make a sound." Julia Ann added, "Daniel slept soundly, but I didn't sleep a wink all night."

✭   ✭   ✭

He was a very successful rancher. He and his sons would buy

cattle in East Texas for $4 per head and then drive them to the railroad's beef pens at Lecompte. They were then shipped to the northern railheads were they would fetch $40, and more per head.

Once, on a cattle drive from Texas, in 1898, the cattle stampeded in the woods. His youngest son Randall Lee, who was only twelve at the time and riding drag, thought his father had been killed. But, then he saw his father's huge white hat waving high in the air, in front of the cattle. Daniel Hubbard Willis Jr. was the author's great-grandfather.

Reverend Daniel Hubbard Willis Sr.–Great-Grandson of Reverend Joseph Willis and father of Daniel Hubbard Willis Jr. He established more churches than Joseph Willis did. He is buried, along with his wife Anna Slaughter Willis, in the Amiable Baptist Church Cemetery. He was blind the last twenty-two years of his life. His daughter would read the scriptures and he would preach. He was the author's 2nd great-grandfather.

Joseph Willis–Preached the first Evangelical sermon West of the Mississippi River, in 1798. He was born into slavery. His mother was Cherokee and his father a wealthy English plantation owner in Bladen County, North Carolina. Joseph swam the mighty Mississippi River at Natchez, at the peril of his own life, riding a mule! He was the author's 4th great-grandfather.

Julia Ann Graham Willis–Wife of Daniel Hubbard Willis Jr. Daughter of Robert Graham. She would often read her red-lettered Bible, eat an orange, including the peel. When she looked at Daniel's Civil War photo tears would come to her eyes.

When asked about eating orange peels by her grandchildren she replied, "I don't know for sure, but I think they're good for you." She was bitten by a ground rattler, at age seventy-five, and survived with home remedies. She swam in Barber Creek, twice a day, until age ninety. She said that was what had prolonged her life. All her children and grandchildren loved to go swimming with her.

According to her granddaughter Ilie Close, "She always had food cooked for family and friends. There was lots of blackberries, huckleberries, and fruit of all kinds for good pies. She was reared a Methodist but later joined the Baptist Church, and was a devoted

Christian. We use to joke, she didn't think there would be anyone but Baptists in Heaven. Her hobby was making quilts and she kept the family supplied with her handiwork." She was the author's great-grandmother.

Randall "Ran" Lee Willis–Youngest child of Daniel Hubbard Willis Jr. and Julia Ann Graham Willis. Named after General Randall Lee Gibson. He married Lillie Gertrude Hanks. He learned to play the fiddle, by ear, after his father bought him one in East Texas, on a cattle drive. He was known to be the very best musician in the area. He was the author's grandfather, whom he was named after.

Henry Elwa Willis–Eldest son of Daniel Hubbard Willis Jr. and Julia Ann Graham Willis. He is buried in the Paul Cemetery, in Lecompte. He named one of his eight children Kit Carson Willis after the famous dime-novel scout. He was the author's great-uncle.

Daniel Oscar Willis, M.D–Son of Daniel Hubbard Willis Jr. and Julia Ann Graham Willis. His father died at his home in Leesville while being treated for Bright's Disease, known as Kidney Disease today. He began his medical practice in 1904, and was the first medical doctor in Vernon Parish. He owned the first automobile in the Parish. He served in United States Army Medical Corps in World War I. He owned the Hotel Leesville. After being slandered by a young lawyer in a trial he bodily removed the lawyer from his room at the Hotel Leesville and then threw him into the street. The young lawyer's name was Huey P. Long. Daniel Oscar Willis was the author's great-uncle.

Ella Willis–Wife of Daniel Oscar Willis, M.D. Born Ella Elizabeth Lamberth.

Robert Kenneth Willis–Son of Daniel Hubbard Willis Jr. and Julia Ann Graham Willis. His wife Eulah Rosalie Hilburn died February 6, 1919, at age thirty-four, during the influenza pandemic of 1918-1919. More people died in the plague than did in World War I. His son Robert Kenneth Willis Jr. was the first casualty from Rapides Parish, in World War II. He's entombed in the USS Arizona, at the bottom of Pearl Harbor. Robert Kenneth Willis was the author's great-uncle.

Eulah Rosalie Hilburn–Wife of Robert Kenneth Willis. Died February 6, 1919, at the age of thirty-four, in the influenza pandemic of 1918-1919. She was recognized as extremely beautiful by everyone.

David Eugene Willis–Son of Daniel Hubbard Willis Jr. and Julia Ann Graham Willis. He died of appendicitis at the age of eight. He was the author's great-uncle.

Stella and Corine Willis–Infant children of Daniel Hubbard Willis Jr. and Julia Ann Graham Willis. Stella lived 111 days and Corine nine days They were the author's great-aunts.

Lillie Gertrude Hanks–Wife of Randall "Ran" Lee Willis. They married on January 11, 1914. She was sixteen and he was twenty-seven. They had three sons: Howard, Herman, and Julian (the author's father). She was the author's sainted grandmother and the wellspring of many of his stories.

Mary Stark Hanks–Mother of Lillie Gertrude Hanks Willis. She traveled with her parents John and Celina Marie Deroussel Stark, by covered wagon, to Branch, Louisiana. After the birth of six children and the premature death of her first husband Charles Oliver she married Arthur Allen Hanks. They had five children. He abandoned her and their children. She was the author's maternal great-grandmother.

Arthur Allen Hanks–Husband of Mary Stark Hanks. He was seventeen-years younger than her and the father of Lillie Gertrude Hanks. He deserted her and their five children for a woman twenty-three years younger than him. They fled to the Indian Territory and lived near Quay and Yale, Oklahoma. He is buried in the Lawson Cemetery north of Yale, Oklahoma, in an unmarked grave. He was the author's maternal great-grandfather.

Jeremiah and Jacob Stark–Based upon Mary Stark Hank's brothers Rufus and Thomas Stark. Their stories in this book are purely fictional.

Matthew Willis–Brother of Daniel Hubbard Willis Jr. He fell in love with Julia Ann Graham Willis's sister Lucy Ruth Graham. She didn't feel the same way.

Lucy Ruth Graham–Youngest sister of Julia Ann Graham Willis. She married James Moore. She died at age forty-two and is buried in the Moore Cemetery, near Forest Hill.

Boss Man Jake–Based upon Julian "Jake" Willis. He was the author's father.

Jimbo–Based upon Jimmy "Jimbo" Matheson. He is a friend of the author.

William Graham–Son of Robert Graham and brother of Julia Ann Graham. His gravestone, in Butters Cemetery, near Forest Hill, has KKK inscribed on it.

Gerald Duke–A cowboy's cowboy. He was known as Jerry Duke. His last horse was named Majestic. He was the author's brother. As boys, they would work as a team roping, branding, and herding cattle.

Jim Bowie–Famous for his knife as well as fighting to defend the Alamo. He was a slave trader and a neighbor of Joseph Willis.

Charlie Goodnight–The best known rancher in Texas history. Historian J. Frank Dobie wrote, "Goodnight approached greatness more nearly than any other cowman of history."

Richard King–**Riverman**, steamboat entrepreneur, livestock capitalist, and founder of the King Ranch. Some believe his ghost wanders the halls of the Menger Hotel, in San Antonio.

Ozeme Carriere–Leader of the most notorious band of Jayhawkers in Louisiana during the Civil War.

General Randall Lee Gibson–Confederate general in the Civil War. He was a member of the House of Representatives and U.S. Senator from Louisiana. He was a founder of Tulane University. The author's grandfather, Randall Lee Willis, was named after him. The author was named after his grandfather.

General Nathaniel Banks–Union general in the Civil War. After occupying Alexandria he advanced up the Red River only to be halted by Confederate forces. In retreat Banks and his men burned ninety percent of Alexandria.

Shanghai Pierce–One of the most colorful cattlemen in early Texas history. He trailed cattle to Louisiana, in 1855. In 1900, Pierce lost more than $1.25 million in the Galveston hurricane. He died three months later. The Pierce estate imported Brahman cattle from India which furnished Texas with the base stock from which large herds of Brahmans have grown.

Henry Warmoth–Governor of Louisiana was widely considered a "carpetbagger," a northerner who moved to the South after the Civil War.

Jean Lafitte–French-American pirate and privateer in the Gulf of Mexico in the early 19th century. He supplied men, weapons, and his knowledge of the region during the battle of New Orleans which helped General Andrew Jackson to secure an overwhelming victory.

Captain J. F. Gerard–School Teacher in Louisiana turned bandit.

Appendix B

About Babb's Bridge, Louisiana

Babb's Bridge was the home of Joseph Willis, in 1828, although it was not known by any name then, other than Joseph Willis's home. It later became his great-grandson Daniel Hubbard Willis's home and then his son and the author's grandfather Randall Lee Willis's home. It was located three miles, as the crow flies, from Amiable Baptist Church (established by Joseph Willis, in 1828) and a little over a mile from present-day Longleaf, Louisiana. Longleaf is less than three miles from Forest Hill.

Babb's Bridge was a community of a few stores and homes and the location of a pine bridge spanning Spring Creek (the headwaters to Cocodrie Lake) in Civil War times. It also had a post office named Lucky Hit and a schoolhouse named Spring Creek Academy (later moved and renamed Spring Hill Academy).

Not so long ago, the water was so clear that you could read a book at its bottom, however, later pollution became a serious problem due to sand and gravel extraction. In 1996, two Louisiana environmental groups, the Sierra Club and Louisiana Environmental Action Network filed a lawsuit, in Federal Court, against the United States Environmental Protection Agency (EPA) to stop it. They did, but the damage had been done.

Catharine Cole wrote, in 1892, in *Louisiana Voyages: The Travel Writings of Catharine Cole*, "There is a little thirty-year-old town by the name of Babb's Bridge. The bridge, Babb's Bridge you know is an affair of scented pine planks that steeply roofs over a section of the lovely creek, so clear, so pure, that if one cast a newspaper on its shingly bottom I quite believe one could read its pages through the spectacles of the water." She added, "I was told of an orchard at this place where the pears weigh a pound each." And, "We put by the ponies at Babb's Bridge and I went by invitation to the schoolhouse."

The site of the long-extinct community is just off Louisiana

Highway 165. It can best be found by traveling Boy Scout Road a short distance of three-fourths of a mile to a pipeline right-a-way, on the left, between Myers Road and Willis Gunter Road. The pipeline right-a-way leads directly down to the location of where the bridge once was.

The location of Daniel Hubbard Willis's home, known as the Ole Willis Place, was located on Barber Creek. There is a huge gravel pit and sand dunes next to where the home once stood. It was located on present-day Willis Gunter Road, near Boy Scout Road. Barber Creek flows into Spring Creek near the old community of Babb's Bridge.

Appendix C

The Birth of the Books and the Play

As a child Randy Willis lived on Barber Creek near Longleaf and Forest Hill, Louisiana. As a teenager, he would work cows with his family there on the open range, owned by lumber companies. Seven generations of his family have lived there, beginning with his 4th Great-Grandfather, Joseph Willis. He would often ride his horse through his family's neighboring property, which was once William Prince Ford's Wallfield Plantation, not realizing the significance of his ancestor's connection to Solomon Northup and William Prince Ford.

After writing many articles and the biography *The Apostle to the Opelousas*, Randy Willis got the idea for the novels *Twice a Slave*, *Three Winds Blowing*, *Louisiana Wind*, and the play *Twice a Slave* from his friend and fellow historian Dr. Sue Eakin. She contacted him after reading an article that mentioned he had obtained the Spring Hill Baptist Church minutes. The minutes had much information on two of its founders: Joseph Willis and William Prince Ford.

Ford had bought the slave Solomon Northup on June 23, 1841, in New Orleans. He immediately brought him to his Wallfield Plantation. Just forty-six days later, Joseph Willis and William Prince Ford founded Spring Hill Baptist Church, on August 8, 1841. Ford's slaves attended the church too, which was the custom in pre-Civil War Louisiana.

The plantation was located on Hurricane Creek, a fourth-mile east of present-day Forest Hill, Louisiana. It was located on the crest of a hill, on the Texas Road that ran along side a ridge. Northup called this area, in his book *Twelve Years a Slave*, "The Great Piney Woods." Ford was also the headmaster of Spring Creek Academy located near his plantation and Spring Hill Baptist Church. It was there, in 1841, that Joseph Willis would live and entrust his diary to his protégé

William Prince Ford, according to early historian W.E. Paxton.

Ford was not a Baptist preacher when he purchased Solomon Northup and the slave Eliza, a.k.a. Dradey, in 1841, as many books, articles, blogs, and the movie *12 Years a Slave* have portrayed.

The first part of the Spring Hill Baptist Church minutes are written in Ford's own handwriting since he was the church 's first secretary and also the first church clerk. The minutes reveal that on July 7, 1842, Ford was elected deacon. On December 11, 1842, Ford became the church 's treasurer, too. It was during the winter of 1842 that Ford sold a 60% share of Northup to John M. Tibeats. Ford's remaining 40% was later conveyed to Edwin Epps, on April 9, 1843.

It was not until February 10, 1844, that Ford was ordained as a Baptist preacher. A year later, on April 12, 1845, Ford was excommunicated for "communing with the Campbellite Church at Cheneyville." But, Ford's later writings reveal that he remained close friends with his neighbor and mentor Joseph Willis.

*   *   *

Dr. Sue Eakin asked Randy Willis if he would help her with her research on William Prince Ford. He also lectured in her history classes, at Louisiana State University at Alexandria, on the subject.

Dr. Eakin wrote Randy Willis on March 7, 1984, "We had a wonderful experience dramatizing Northup and I think there could be a musical play on Joseph Willis. It seems to me it gets the message across far more quickly than routine written material." She added, "a fictional novel based upon Joseph Willis's life would be more interesting to the general public than a biography and would reach a greater audience."

Dr. Eakin is best known for documenting, annotating, and reviving interest in Solomon Northup's 1853 book *Twelve Years a Slave*. She, at the age of eighteen, rediscovered a long-forgotten copy of Solomon Northup's book, on the shelves of a bookstore, near the LSU campus, in Baton Rouge. The bookstore owner sold it to her for only 25 cents. In 2013, *12 Years a Slave* won the Academy Award for Best Picture.

In his acceptance speech for the honor, director Steve McQueen thanked Dr. Eakin: "I'd like to thank this amazing historian, Sue Eakin, whose life, she gave her life's work to preserving Solomon's book."

James "Jim " Bowie was a neighbor of Joseph Willis when they both lived near Bayou Chicot. Jim's brother, Rezin Bowie, was a neighbor to Joseph's eldest son Agerton Willis and eldest grandson, Daniel Hubbard Willis Sr., for four years (1824-1827) in the village of Bayou Boeuf. The name changed to Holmesville in 1834, and is located near present-day Eola. It was at Holmesville, on Bayou Boeuf, that Edwin Epps enslaved (1845-1853) Solomon Northup for the last eight years of his twelve year indenture. It was there that Joseph's eldest son and Randy Willis's 3rd great-grandfather Agerton Willis met and married a former Irish orphan Sophie Story.

About the Author

Randy Willis is the author of *Three Winds Blowing, Louisiana Wind, Light, The Apostle to the Opelousas, The Story of Joseph Willis*, and is co-author of *Twice a Slave*. *Twice a Slave* has been chosen as a Jerry B. Jenkins Select Book, along with four bestselling authors. Jerry Jenkins is author of more than 180 books with sales of more than 70 million copies, including the best-selling *Left Behind* series.

Twice a Slave has been adapted into a dramatic play at Louisiana College, by Dr. D. "Pete" Richardson (Associate Professor of Theater with Louisiana College).

He owns Randy Willis Music Publishing (an ASCAP-affiliated music publishing company), and Town Lake Music Publishing, LLC (a BMI-affiliated music publishing company). He is an ASCAP-affiliated songwriter.

He is the founder of Operation Warm Heart, which feeds and clothes the homeless, and is a member of the Board of Directors of Our Mission Possible (empowering at-risk teens to discover their greatness) in Austin, Texas. He is a member of the Board of Trustees of the Joseph Willis Institute at Louisiana College.

Randy Willis was born in Oakdale, Louisiana, and lived near Forest Hill and Longleaf, Louisiana, on Barber Creek, as a boy. He currently resides in the Texas Hill Country. He graduated from Angleton High School in Angleton, Texas, and Texas State University in San Marcos, Texas, with a BBA. He was a graduate student at Texas State University. He is single and the father of three sons and has four grandchildren. He is a fourth great-grandson of Joseph Willis, and his foremost historian.

Author's Note

Many of the fictional events in these pages are inspired by stories passed down through my ancestors. A few are influenced with cowboy stories from long ago. Others are a combination of all of the above with a heavy dose of my own imagination. Most have an accurate historical timeline and background. In some cases I chose to use the most recent names of towns rather than their 1800s counterparts. For instance Mayflower, Texas, was originally known as Survey, or Surveyville. Forest Hill, Louisiana, didn't officially become a town until 1897.

On the other hand I used Babb's Bridge's 1800s name because it no longer exists by any name.

My Great-Grandfather Daniel Hubbard Willis Jr. is the primary character in this book. He was fifteen at the time of his great-grandfather Joseph Willis's death. My grandfather Randall "Ran" Lee Willis was his youngest son. I was named after him.

His father was Reverend Daniel Hubbard Willis Sr. He was the first descendant of Joseph Willis to follow him into the ministry. Daniel Sr. was the eldest son of Joseph's eldest son Agerton Willis. He was almost thirty-seven at the time of Joseph's death.

These stories are inspired by our family's history passed down through these men and woman in the 19th century and then to their descendants on into the 21st century. Joseph Willis's legacy has influenced each generation of our family and many others, too.

It is my desire and goal that readers will discover the importance of passing along family history, traditions, and stories that will serve to teach the next generation.

* * *

To learn more about the characters
in this book visit:
www.threewindsblowing.com